Hello, Family Members,

Learning to read is one of the most i[mportant]  of early childhood. **Hello Reader!** b[ooks help] children become skilled readers wh[...] readers learn to read by remember[ing] words like "the," "is," and "and"; by using phonics skills to decode new words; and by interpreting picture and text clues. These books provide both the stories children enjoy and the structure they need to read fluently and independently. Here are suggestions for helping your child *before*, *during*, and *after* reading:

Before

• Look at the cover and pictures and have your child predict what the story is about.
• Read the story to your child.
• Encourage your child to chime in with familiar words and phrases.
• Echo read with your child by reading a line first and having your child read it after you do.

During

• Have your child think about a word he or she does not recognize right away. Provide hints such as "Let's see if we know the sounds" and "Have we read other words like this one?"
• Encourage your child to use phonics skills to sound out new words.
• Provide the word for your child when more assistance is needed so that he or she does not struggle and the experience of reading with you is a positive one.
• Encourage your child to have fun by reading with a lot of expression . . . like an actor!

After

• Have your child keep lists of interesting and favorite words.
• Encourage your child to read the books over and over again. Have him or her read to brothers, sisters, grandparents, and even teddy bears. Repeated readings develop confidence in young readers.
• Talk about the stories. Ask and answer questions. Share ideas about the funniest and most interesting characters and events in the stories.

I do hope that you and your child enjoy this book.

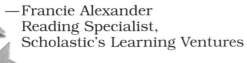

—Francie Alexander
   Reading Specialist,
   Scholastic's Learning Ventures

For my teatime pal, Linda
— J.M.

Computer art for craft instruction pages by Bill Hoffman.
Cut-paper photography by Paul Dyer.

Copyright © 2000 by Judith Moffatt.
All rights reserved. Published by Scholastic Inc.
SCHOLASTIC, HELLO READER, CARTWHEEL BOOKS and associated logos
are trademarks and/or registered trademarks of Scholastic Inc.

Library of Congress Cataloging-in-Publication Data
Moffatt, Judith.
    Snow Shapes : a read-and-do book / by Judith Moffatt.
        p.   cm.— (Hello reader! Level 2)
    Summary: Minky and his friend Mouse provide instructions for making
various paper snowflakes, holiday flowers, and other crafts related to winter.
    ISBN 0-439-09858-0
    1. Paper work—Juvenile literature. 2. Winter in art—Juvenile literature.
[1. Paper work. 2. Handicraft. 3. Winter in art.] I. Title. II. Series.
TT870.M5293   2000
745.594'1—dc21
                                                                99-29208
                                                                   CIP
12   11   10   9   8   7   6   5   4   3   2   1   0/0   01   02   03   04

Printed in the U.S.A.   24
First printing, January 2000

Snow Shapes
A READ-AND-DO BOOK

by Judith Moffatt

Hello Reader! —Level 2

SCHOLASTIC INC.

New York   Toronto   London   Auckland   Sydney
Mexico City   New Delhi   Hong Kong

Minky and Mouse
are playing outside.
They watch the
snowflakes fall.

It's getting cold.
Let's go inside
and make snowflakes
for the wall!

Every snowflake has six sides.

Each one is a different shape.

SNOWFLAKE

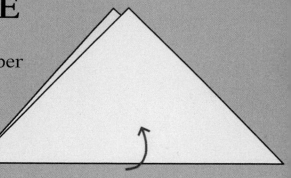

1. Fold a square of paper
   in half to make
   a triangle.

2. Fold the right-hand corner up and across.
   Fold the left-hand corner up and across.

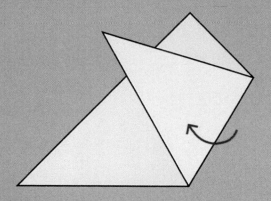

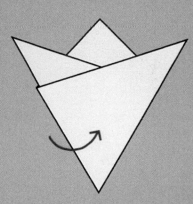

3. Fold your shape
   in half as shown.

4. Cut off the top
   as shown. Keep
   the bottom shape.

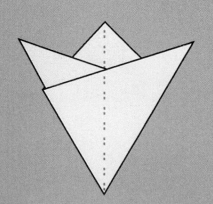

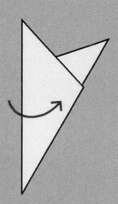

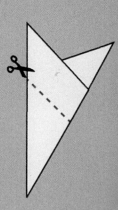

5. Cut and hole punch shapes out of all three sides as shown.

6. Unfold your snowflake!

With a fold and a snip, they are easy and quick. How many will you make?

Our favorite bird
is the cardinal.
His feathers are
brilliant red.

CARDINAL

1. Fold a piece of paper in half.

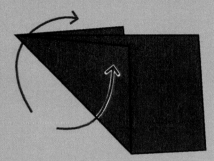

2. Fold the bottom left-hand corner up to meet the center fold. Repeat this fold on the other side.

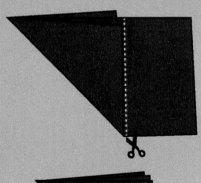

3. Cut off the side as shown. Keep the triangle shape.

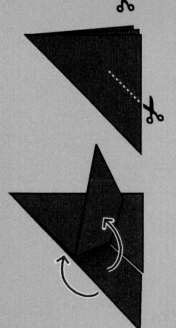

4. Make a cut through the thickness of paper as shown.

5. Fold one side of the paper up to make a wing. Repeat this fold on the other side.

6. Cut out a triangle shape to make the head as shown. Add a black triangle with a white, hole-punched eye.

This bird can sit by your window, or glide with a bit of thread.

Squirrels nibble on nuts they stored before snow covered the ground.

SQUIRRELS

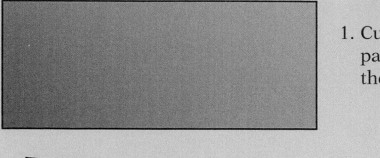

1. Cut a piece of paper in half the long way.

2. Fold the paper in half.

3. Fold one end inward to meet center fold. Repeat this fold on the other side.

Glue acorns to your paper chain,

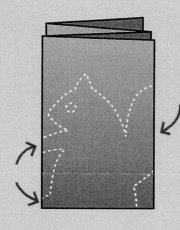

4. Draw a squirrel on one square. Be sure arm, foot, and tail are drawn off the page. The arm and foot should face the fold.

5. Cut out squirrel. Hole punch an eye.

6. Make two paper acorns and glue them between the squirrels' arms.

to show what these friends found.

Who doesn't like a snowman?
Big snowballs piled in stacks.

SNOWMAN

1. Cut out a small, a medium and a large circle using cups, cans, or coins to trace the shapes.

2. Glue these together in a stack as shown.

3. Cut out paper shapes to make a hat, a nose, and arms. Use a hole punch to make eyes and buttons.

4. Glue them all onto your snowman.

5. Punch a hole in his hat and add string.

6. Hang up your snowman!

Let's add some eyes,
a carrot nose,
and a nice top hat of black.

Holiday flowers
are everywhere,

some red, some pink,
some white.

HOLIDAY FLOWERS

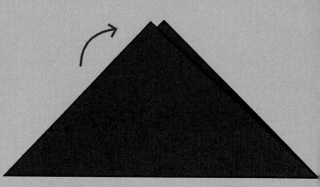

1. Fold a square of paper in half to make a triangle.

2. Fold one point up to the center. Repeat fold with the other point.

3. Fold shape in half again.

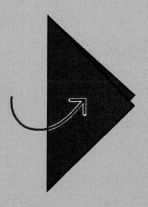

4. Punch a hole near the corner. Cut out a diamond shape as shown.

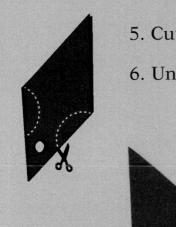

5. Cut out two half circles as shown.

6. Unfold your flower!

Make a garden of these
in your window
for a cheery winter sight.

We hope we gave you
new ideas,

and you learned
a thing or two.

Now you can make
great paper shapes
with scissors, hole punch,
tape, and glue.

Minky and Mouse
are planning new crafts
for you to make real soon.
They work away
on a snowy day
and whistle a happy tune.